To all the adults and parents who value the importance of teaching children about eating a healthy diet that includes fruits and vegetables.

www.mascotbooks.com

For more information, please contact:
Mascot Books
560 Herndon Parkway #120
Herndon, VA 20170
info@mascotbooks.com

Library of Congress Control Number: 2015913306
CPSIA Code: PRT1015A
ISBN-13: 978-1-63177-285-6

Printed in the United States

EMILY AND MAX

By Lauren Rebello

Illustrations by Kent Cairncross

THE SPY INGREDIENT

Max and Emily were playing in the toy room when they started to get a little hungry.

"Mom's in the kitchen, Max," said Emily.

"Ooh... how exciting! Hopefully she is making a smoothie!" replied Max.

"What do you think she will put into the smoothie this time?" asked Emily.

"I don't know, but I sure hope she adds blueberries."

"That would be so yummy, I hope she adds strawberries and—"

"Max! Emily! Please come to the kitchen," called Mom.

Max and Emily raced down the stairs, excited to see what ingredients Mom used in their smoothies this time.

"Let's see if you can guess the secret ingredient," Mom chuckled.

Max and Emily saw no clues on the counter, only the blender with the smoothie already mixed. *Oh boy, no clues to help us guess*, they thought to themselves.

"I hope I guess them all!"
Emily said as she hopped into
her chair.

Maybe it's the blueberries I like, Max hoped as he sat in his
chair. He tried to remember all the ingredients Mom bought
the last time they were at the store.

Mom saw how excited they were to try the smoothie, so she quickly gave them each a cup. "The one clue I'll give you is that one of the ingredients is a spy ingredient!"

"What's a spy ingredient?" asked Max and Emily.

Mom smiled. "A spy ingredient is something you can't see or taste. It blends right in with the other ingredients."

Looking very serious, Max tried another sip of the smoothie. *Is that blueberries I taste?* he wondered. "It tastes like a banana so I know you put bananas in it, Mom."

"You are both right.
Great job guessing!
What else can you taste?
Or see?" asked Mom.

Emily looked at her smoothie, hoping she would see the shape or color of the fruits that were in it. *Blending things together sure makes it hard to guess what they are!* she thought.

Max remembered the apple juice they bought at the store the other day. *Mom always added juice to the smoothies. Mom also bought blackberries, and she loves adding those,* thought Max.

"Mom, I know the juice you used... it's the apple juice we bought together. I bet you used the blackberries too!" Max exclaimed.

"Good thinking, Max. Yes, I used the apple juice to make the ingredients into a drink and the blackberries to add extra vitamins."

"There are three ingredients left for you to guess," said Mom.

Max closed his eyes, sipped the smoothie, and concentrated really hard to figure out what he tasted.

Max's face lit up. "Blueberries, I can taste them. There are blueberries in this!"

"You guessed it Max! Now just one more ingredient to guess."

This time they both closed their eyes as they sipped their smoothies and concentrated as hard as they could. Emily kept thinking about how tasty the smoothie was. She loved the taste of the blueberries, mangoes, bananas, and apple juice.

Max enjoyed the way the smoothie tasted. Instead of thinking of the missing ingredient, he thought about what else he and Mom bought at the store.

"Is it a potato? Mom, the last ingredient is a potato," said Max.

Mom giggled, "No, Max. It is not a potato."

"Max, that would not taste good in a smoothie. Besides I like my potatoes baked, not blended," said Emily. She giggled too.

Max did not giggle; he kept looking seriously at the almost-empty cup.

"Mom, I don't taste anything else," said a frustrated Max.

"And I definitely don't see any clues in here," added Emily as she stared at her half-empty cup.

Max went to the sink to put his cup away. As he threw away his paper towel, he noticed some green leaves in the trash. *What else did we buy at the store...?* thought Max.

"Spinach! Mom, is the spy ingredient spinach?"

"Max, why did you guess that?" asked Emily as she looked in her cup. "I don't see anything green in here, or taste any leaves."

"That's exactly why spinach is the spy ingredient!" said Mom. "When it's mixed in a fruit smoothie, you can't taste or see it.

"It's like a spy, nobody knows it's there!" they both exclaimed.

"Thanks for making a smoothie, Mom," said Max.

"Yes, guessing ingredients is so much fun!" added Emily.

"Yes it is fun," replied Mom. "Plus, you get a lot of the vitamins you both need to build a healthy body."

About the Author

Lauren Rebello is a Registered Nurse with ten years of nursing experience. Maintaining an optimal healthy lifestyle has always been a priority to her. She was inspired to create a way to encourage kids to eat healthier when she noticed a decreased interest in eating fruits and vegetables with her children, Malkolm and Emma. When she sparked their interest in drinking smoothies by asking them to guess the ingredients, they immediately had an increased desire to have smoothies. This meant they would have more fruits and vegetables in their daily diet. She is currently working on the next book to be published in the *Max and Emily* series.

Please visit the author's website at:
www.EmilyandMaxSeries.com.